characters created by
lauren child

But excuse me THAT is My book

the transparent library and some annoying flies

PUFFIN

Text based on script written by Bridget Hurst and Carol Noble

Illustrations from the TV animation produced by Tiger Aspect

With special thanks to Leigh Hodgkinson

PUFFIN BOOKS
Published by the Penguin Group: London, New York, Australia,
Canada, India, Ireland, New Zealand and South Africa
Penguin Books Ltd, Registered Offices: 80 Strand, London WC2R 0RL, England

puffinbooks.com

First published 2005
This edition published 2008
1 3 5 7 9 10 8 6 4 2

Made and printed in China
ISBN 978-1-856-13182-7

This edition produced for The Book People Ltd,
Hall Wood Avenue, Haydock, St Helens WA11 9UL

I have this little sister Lola.
She is small and very funny.
Lola loves reading and she really loves books.
But at the moment there is
one book that is extra specially special.

One day, Lola said,
    "Charlie, Dad says he will take
us to the library and we must go
    right now and get
        Beetles, Bugs and Butterflies."

Lola loves Beetles, Bugs and Butterflies.

I say,
    "But Dad took that book out
            for you last time...
And the time before that..."

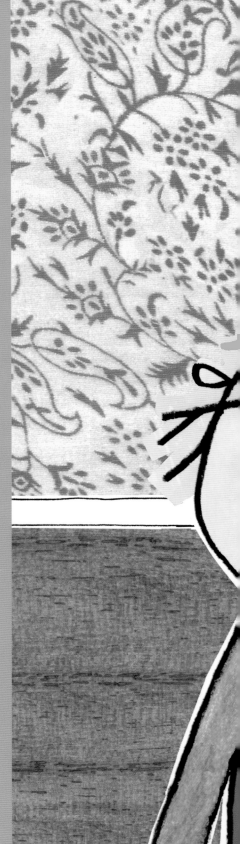

Then Lola says,
    "But Charlie, Beetles, Bugs and Butterflies is a very special book that is my favourite and I really need it.

Now.

    Now.

        Now.

        Now.

            Now!

Don't you know Beetles, Bugs and Butterflies is the best book in the whole world?"

And Lola says,

"You see, Charlie,

the bugs are quite buggy

and the butterflies are really beautiful and

the beetles are...

very silly.

The beetle gets stuck!
And his legs are very funny!

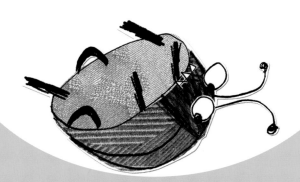

And he

can't

get

down!"

I say,
"I know that, Lola.
Come on.
Dad's waiting."

"All his funny
little legs. Charlie!"

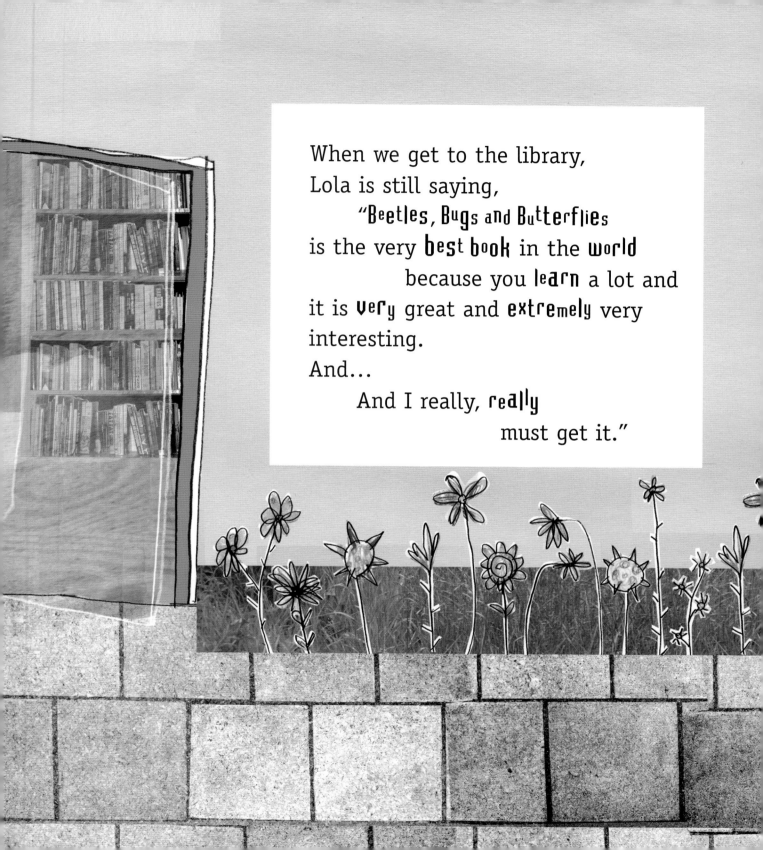

When we get to the library,
Lola is still saying,
　　"Beetles, Bugs and Butterflies
is the very best book in the world
　　　　because you learn a lot and
it is very great and extremely very
interesting.
And...
　　　And I really, really
　　　　　　must get it."

When we get inside
I have to say,

"Shh! Lola, it's a library.
We have to be quiet."

Lola says,
"But I can't find
my book, Charlie."

And I say,
"Then why don't you
try looking for it

with all the books
beginning with **B**?"

So Lola says,

"B, B, B... Where is my book?
Where can it be?"

I say, "Lola! Be quiet!"

She says,

"I am being quiet, Charlie!"

I say, "Shhhhh!"

She says, "I am shushing!
It's not there!
My book's not there!"

I say, "Lola! Be quiet!"
Lola says, "But Charlie, My book is lost!
It is completely not there!"

I say,
"Lola, remember this is a library
so someone must have borrowed it."

Lola says,
"But Beetles, Bugs
and Butterflies
is My book."

I say,
"But it's not your library.
Someone else obviously
wanted to read your book."

Lola says,
"But they can't. It's My book."

So I say, "Lola, just think.
There are hundreds and hundreds of other books
in the library to choose from.

There are spy books and dinosaur books. Adventure books

and scary books.

Books about princes,
    aeroplanes and astronauts.

Books about castles,
    dragons and volcanoes,

monsters,

mountains and pixies.   And books about Romans."

Romersk

فورح

România

I say,
"Look! Romans! This one tells you
　　　all about history in the Roman times.
Like how the Romans built long, straight roads
　　　and rode chariots and had
　　　fights with swords."

oma`li

umi

римский

ro-man

римски

római

로마

Römer

zymski

Rómv

România

latinluk

But Lola says,
"Too many
big
words,
Charlie.

So I say,
"OK, Lola, let's try to find
a book with more pictures and less words.

How about this? An encyclopedia?
It's got millions of drawings and millions of facts.
You can learn about **everything**.
Look, this page is all about helicopters."

I say,
"You might be right, Lola,
but see what you
think of this...
It's a pop-up book."

But Lola says,
"A book that ha

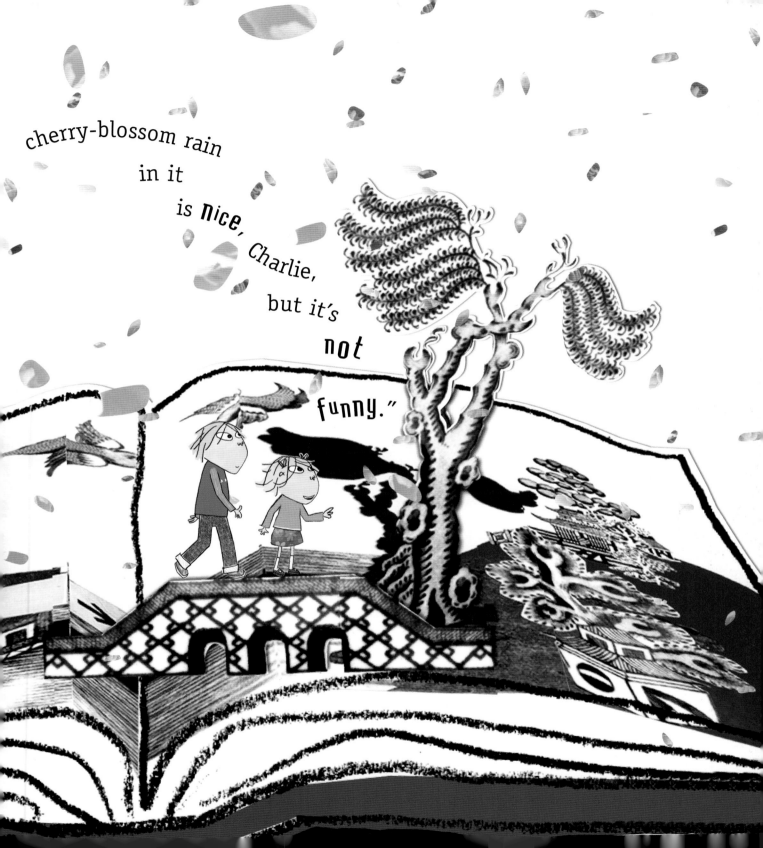

cherry-blossom rain
in it
is nice, Charlie,
but it's
not
funny."

Then Lola says,
"Beetles, Bugs and Butterflies
is really funny
and makes me

laugh

and

laugh

and

laugh..."

I say,
"So it's an **animal** book you want.
         A book with... lots of pictures... a story...
no **big** words... and animals that make you laugh."
         Lola says, "Yep."
I say, "How about this, Lola?! Cheetahs and Chimpanzees."
         Lola says, "Are there
beetles, bugs and butterflies in it?!"
         I say, "No, there are
cheetahs and chimpanzees.
Give it a try, Lola. Please."

Lola says, "OK, Charlie,
         I will. But it won't
be as good as...

Beetles,
Bugs
and
Butterflies!

Oh no, Charlie! Look!
That girl's got My book!
I don't think she knows
it is
My book!

No, n0O...

Just wait...

That's **my**...

That's **my**...

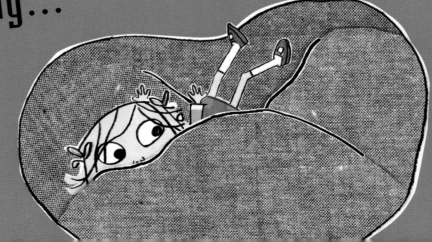

I
just
like
My book,
Charlie!"

Lola says,
"I want **my book**, Charlie!"
And I say,
   "But you said you would try
               Cheetahs and Chimpanzees."

   Lola says,
"Well... I'll try it
            but it won't be as good
         as Beetles, Bugs and Butterflies."

But then Lola says,
"Oh! Look at that. The cheetahs are very fast and the chimpanzees

are very cheeky and in fact, you know what, Charlie...?

This **book** is probably
the **most best book** in the whole wide world
because it is so **interesting** and so **lovely**
and you know it has the **absolutely** best **pictures** of **any book ever**
and the baby **chimps** are very **funny**..."

ISTANBUL

YÜCEL AKAT

Archaeologist

WRITTEN BY	:	YÜCEL AKAT Archaeologist
TRANSLATION	:	MAGGIE PINAR
PHOTOS BY	:	NACİ KESKİN, HALUK ÖZÖZLÜ, TAHSİN AYDOĞMUŞ, SÜHA DERBENT
GRAPHIS BY	:	NURAY ÖZBAL
COLOUR SEPERATION	:	RENK GRAFİK, HANER OFSET
TYPE SET	:	FLASH FOTO DİZGİ
PUBLISHED and PRINTED	:	KESKİN COLOR KARTPOSTALCILIK LTD. ŞTİ. MATBAASI
DISTRIBUTED	:	KESKİN COLOR KARTPOSTALCILIK SAN.ve PAZ. A.Ş. ANKARA CAD. NO 98 34410 SİRKECİ - İSTANBUL TEL: 0 (212) 514 17 47 - 514 17 48 - 514 17 49 FAX : 512 09 64
BRANCH OFFICE	:	KIŞLA MAH. 54. SK. GÜNAYDIN APT. NO.6/B 07040 ANTALYA TEL: 0 (242) 247 15 41 - 247 16 11 FAX: 0 (242) 247 16 11

İSBN 975-7559-10-5

1997
© copyright by KESKİN COLOR AŞ